Slow Doris

Maverick
Early Readers

'Slow Doris'
An original concept by Steve Howson
© Steve Howson

Illustrated by Kristen Humphrey

Published by MAVERICK ARTS PUBLISHING LTD
Studio 11, City Business Centre, 6 Brighton Road,
Horsham, West Sussex, RH13 5BB
© Maverick Arts Publishing Limited November 2020
+44 (0)1403 256941

A CIP catalogue record for this book is available at the British Library.

ISBN 978-1-84886-720-8

www.maverickbooks.co.uk

This book is rated as: Gold Band (Guided Reading)

Slow Doris

By **Steve Howson**

Illustrated by
Kristen Humphrey

Chapter 1

Doris was a loris. A very slow loris.

Boris and Horace were lorises too. But they were always rushing around. When they said, 'come and race with us', Doris would always say, 'no thank you'.

"But you're missing out on all the fun," said Boris. "Everyone loves the midnight jungle races. All the animals cheer and there's

always a party afterwards."

Boris and Horace were famous in the jungle races.

Doris preferred to be by herself. She didn't like the noise and the crowds. She liked to do things at her own pace. "When you go slow," she said, "you see so much more."

Like the hairs on a petal.

Like crystals twinkling in a rock.

Like wriggling tadpoles clinging to a leaf.

Like the swirly patterns inside your eyelids...

"Doris, wake up," cried Boris. "You're such a night-dreamer. Save your sleeping for the daytime, like the rest of us."

But Doris stayed out of the races. She didn't go to the parties. She avoided the noise and the crowds. She stayed up in her tree, night-dreaming alone.

Chapter 2

One night, when Doris was busy watching the leaves grow, she heard a strange noise.

It came from down below. It was harsh and grumbly.

She peered over the edge of her nest and saw two bright lights sweeping through the jungle. She could hear something big and heavy crashing around.

There was shouting and commotion.
Then she saw a great square creature with
red eyes bouncing out of the jungle and
rushing away over the hill.

The jungle fell silent for a moment.

Then there was a shrill cry. It was Cloris the
loris. "Boris and Horace have gone!" she
screamed.

Doris slowly crept down from her tree, peering into the darkness.

Cloris came rushing past. "Quick, Doris," she said. "Help us find Boris and Horace."

All the lorises were rushing around in a panic.

"Did you see that big square creature with red eyes?" asked Doris.

Nobody listened.

"I think it took Boris and Horace," said Doris.

Cloris snapped, "This is no time for your night-dreams, Doris. Help us find Boris and Horace, or go back to sleep."

Doris started looking around, very slowly. She noticed how the grass had been trampled flat.

She found some broken branches. She saw
strange marks in the mud.

Then she saw tracks she had never seen
before. They led out of the jungle.
Doris followed them.

Chapter 3

Slowly and carefully, Doris followed the tracks over the hill and down the other side.

The sun came up.
Doris kept on following the tracks.

Sometimes, more big square creatures rushed past, spraying dust and stones.

Doris hid in the shadows until they had gone.

She plodded on, with her eyes fixed on the tracks.

The sun beat down on her back. All the other lorises would be asleep by now. Doris had never been out in the daylight before.
She had never been so far from home.

But she kept on going.

Soon it grew cooler. The sun went down.
Doris could still see the tracks in the dust.
So she kept on going.

The moon rose and strange sounds filled
Doris's ears.

Up ahead there were bright lights in the
darkness. They stung Doris's eyes.

As she crept closer, she saw people everywhere. They pushed and shoved and shouted at each other. They didn't notice little Doris down by their feet.

Doris decided to hide in the shadows, until they had gone.

Chapter 4

Eventually, the people started to drift away. Finally, when all was quiet, Doris dared to peep out from her hiding place.

The dusty floor was criss-crossed with tracks like the ones she had been following.

Then she saw it. There, at last, was the big square creature that had crashed into her jungle. It was silent and its red eyes were closed.

Doris also saw that all around there were cages crammed full of jungle animals. There were monkeys and bats, birds and reptiles. They dozed in their cages or stared down at her with sad eyes.

"Doris!" called a voice. "Over here!"

It was Horace. And there was Boris too.

"How did you find us?" called Boris.

"I followed the tracks made by the big square creature," said Doris. Then she climbed up to their cage and started to chew on the ropes that held it together.

"Hurry up, Doris, please," cried Boris.

Doris chewed slowly and steadily, until...

SNAP!

The cage door fell open. Boris and Horace leapt out and gave Doris a great big hug.

"Come on, let's get out of here," said Boris.

"But what about the other animals?" said Doris. "We can't leave them here."

So Doris, Boris and Horace used their sharp teeth to chew through the ropes around the other cages. As the animals were freed, they used their teeth or claws or beaks to help.

By the end of the night, all the animals were free.

"I just have to do one more thing," said Doris.

Boris and Horace watched as she crept over to the big square creature. Its red eyes were still closed.

Boris and Horace held their breath as Doris crawled underneath. She reached up and pulled down a wire. The big square creature did not move. Doris chewed through the wire until it snapped.

Finally, she reached up and bit into a thin pipe. It burst and liquid poured onto the ground.

Doris headed back to Boris and Horace as quickly as she could. "I hope that stops it following us," she said.

The sky was beginning to grow light. Horace said, "Come on! Let's go before those people come back. They won't be very happy."

But Doris was too tired to take another step. She dropped into the dust and fell fast asleep. So Boris and Horace carried her all the way home.

Chapter 5

Doris awoke to the sound of cheering and shouting. She opened her eyes to see hundreds of lorises waving and chanting her name:

"Doris! Doris! Doris!"

Boris and Horace held her up high so everyone could see. There was a huge cheer from the crowd.

"You're the hero now!" cried Cloris from below. "We're having the biggest party ever. Come and join us."

"Thank you," said Doris. "But I'd just like to go back to my tree, if you don't mind."

Doris curled up cosily among the leaves in her nest.

She could hear the distant noise of the party below.

She watched a night flower slowly unfolding.

She listened to the sap pulsing through the leaves as she lay down her head.

It was good to be back in her tree, night-dreaming alone.

The End

Book Bands for Guided Reading

The Institute of Education book banding system is a scale of colours that reflects the various levels of reading difficulty. The bands are assigned by taking into account the content, the language style, the layout and phonics. Word, phrase and sentence level work is also taken into consideration.

Maverick Early Readers are a bright, attractive range of books covering the pink to white bands. All of these books have been book banded for guided reading to the industry standard and edited by a leading educational consultant.

Pink
Red
Yellow
Blue
Green
Orange
Turquoise
Purple
Gold
White

To view the whole Maverick Readers scheme, visit our website at

www.maverickearlyreaders.com

Or scan the QR code above to view our scheme instantly!